SCIENCE DETECTIVE

The
MYSTERIOUS
LIGHTS

and Other Cases

Other Books in the
EINSTEIN ANDERSON,
SCIENCE DETECTIVE Series
by Seymour Simon
from Avon Camelot

ON-LINE SPACEMAN
AND OTHER CASES

THE HOWLING DOG
AND OTHER CASES

THE HALLOWEEN HORROR
AND OTHER CASES

THE GIGANTIC ANTS
AND OTHER CASES

THE TIME MACHINE
AND OTHER CASES

THE WINGS OF DARKNESS
AND OTHER CASES

Coming Soon

THE INVISIBLE MAN
AND OTHER CASES

#6

Einstein Anderson
SCIENCE DETECTIVE

The
MYSTERIOUS
LIGHTS
and Other Cases

Seymour Simon
illustrated by S. D. Schindler

(previously published as *Einstein Anderson Lights Up the Sky*)

AN AVON CAMELOT BOOK

AVON BOOKS, INC.
1350 Avenue of the Americas
New York, New York 10019

Text copyright © 1982, 1998 by Seymour Simon
Interior illustrations copyright © 1998 by S.D. Schindler
Interior illustrations by S.D. Schindler
First published in 1982 by Viking Penguin under the title *Einstein Anderson Lights Up the Sky*
Revised hardcover edition published by Morrow Junior Books in 1998
Published by arrangement with the author
Library of Congress Catalog Card Number: 96-41766
ISBN: 0-380-72660-2
www.avonbooks.com

Published in hardcover by Morrow Junior Books/William Morrow and Company, Inc.; for information address Permissions Department, William Morrow and Company, Inc., 1350 Avenue of the Americas, New York, New York 10019.

First Avon Camelot Printing: April 1999

CAMELOT TRADEMARK REG. U.S. PAT. OFF. AND IN OTHER COUNTRIES, MARCA REGISTRADA, HECHO EN U.S.A.

Printed in the U.S.A.

OPM 10 9 8 7 6 5 4 3 2 1

To the memory of my mother,
Clara Simon

CONTENTS

1

The Case of the

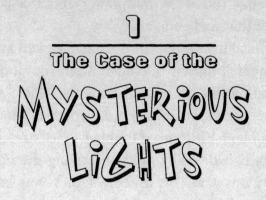

MYSTERIOUS LIGHTS

instein Anderson was in a spaceship, darting down through the atmosphere of a strange new planet. The spaceship shook like a leaf in a storm. The jagged mountain peaks of the planet loomed dangerously close. Einstein quickly shut off the malfunctioning computer and seized the ship's controls. The view screen darkened and...

"Wake up, Einstein," Dennis said, shaking him by the shoulder. "It's time to get up. What kind of dream are you having?" he con-

1

tinued. "You were mumbling about a computer that had gone crazy."

Einstein opened his eyes and looked at his younger brother, Dennis. Then he looked around at his room and shook his head. "As a great professor once said, when in doubt, mumble," Einstein mumbled. He stretched and yawned. "Why are you waking me up so early, anyway?" he asked. "Don't you know today is Saturday?"

"Don't you like to wake up early on Saturday, Einstein?" Dennis asked innocently. "After all, don't you wake me up early every weekday to get ready for school?"

Einstein grinned. "It's my job to wake you up on school days," he said. "But you'd better have a good reason for getting me up so early today."

"I got you up so we can go along with Mom when she interviews those vampire people who are having the world premiere of their movie tonight."

Einstein put on his glasses, which promptly slid down on his nose. He pushed them back with one finger and said, "Right, I remember now. That's the vampire movie that was filmed in Sparta a few months ago, called *Wings of Darkness*. The director even tried to get some publicity by having a phony vampire scare."

"Mom's going to write a column on the premiere, but she wants to go down earlier so she can interview some of the actors and the director," Dennis said. "They're going to have a preview this afternoon for the press, and she can get us in." Mrs. Anderson was an editor and writer for one of the town's newspapers, the Sparta *Tribune*.

"O.K.," Einstein said. "I'll get dressed in double-quick time and meet you in the kitchen. How about mixing up some pancake batter? I'm in the mood for a bit of breakfast."

Einstein's real name was Adam. But few people called him by his given name anymore. That was because he had been interested in science from an early age. His kindergarten teacher began to call him by the nickname of Einstein, after the most famous scientist of this century. By the time he was in second grade, he was solving science problems that stumped even his teachers. Even his parents sometimes called him by his nickname.

Einstein quickly washed and got dressed in his favorite pair of jeans, which were getting raggedy at the knees. He looked out the window at the dark, cloudy skies and chose a warm shirt, his nylon baseball jacket, and a pair of beat-up sneakers. It was just as well that he was going to see the movie this afternoon, Einstein thought. It looked like it was going to be too wet for his baseball game, anyway.

Dr. Anderson, Einstein's father, was making his special weekend omelet when Einstein came down to the kitchen. Dennis was making pancakes, and Mrs. Anderson was pouring orange juice into glasses. Einstein's parents greeted him with affection. Dr. Anderson, a veterinarian, was often out on emergency calls before his sons got up in the morning. It was a treat for all of them to eat together on weekends.

"Dad," said Einstein, "what's yellow, soft, and goes round and round?"

Dr. Anderson looked at his son and

smiled. "I don't know," he said, "but something tells me I'll soon find out."

"A long-playing omelet," said Einstein.

"Ugh," said the other three people in the room.

After Einstein's "bit" of breakfast—pancakes, part of the omelet, orange juice, and a glass of milk to settle everything down—Einstein washed the dishes and cleaned up in the kitchen. It was his turn. Then Mrs. Anderson, Einstein, and Dennis drove over to the Capitol movie theater, where the preview was to take place.

When they arrived, workmen were busy setting up huge spotlights on the roof of the theater, laying down a red carpet leading to the entrance, and setting up wooden barricades to keep back the crowds they expected that evening. Even the Sparta chief of police was there, talking to some of his officers about crowd control.

Mrs. Anderson used her press pass to get them all in and then began her interviews. At first the boys listened, then they wandered around and watched the workmen. Einstein was still a little hungry, so he bought a bag of peanuts, which he shared with his brother. A little later Mrs. Anderson finished the interviews. She took the boys out to lunch. It was drizzling slightly and had gotten colder.

When they came back to the theater in the late afternoon for the press screening, darkness had fallen. But the theater was brightly lit and the searchlights were sweeping back and forth.

They went in and sat down to watch the screening of *Wings of Darkness*. There were only about fifty or sixty people in the audience. Mrs. Anderson pointed out the director, the producer, and some of the actors. Einstein recognized Boris Vlad, who had worked on the lighting for the film. In order to get publicity for the movie, he had claimed he had seen a vampire.

The movie had been filmed in an old mansion in Sparta. Most of the scenes were too dark to show much of the house, but the boys enjoyed the movie, which was quite suspenseful and scary.

When the movie was over, everybody stood around in little groups, talking about the film. Mrs. Anderson introduced Einstein and Dennis to Mr. Freed, the director. Mr. Freed looked worried. He had been talking to the chief of police, who had just left, looking angry.

"Can you imagine that?" said Mr. Freed. "The chief of police is blaming me for the bunch of flying-saucer calls he's been getting in the last hour or two. He says we're getting people to call in to say they have seen UFOs

so that we can get publicity for the movie. He says if he doesn't stop getting the calls he's going to cancel the premiere."

"Well, you can hardly blame him," said

Mrs. Anderson. "You *did* arrange those earlier stories about a vampire to get publicity."

"Yeah, but your son found us out." Mr. Freed looked at Einstein. "Listen, kid," he said, "we really have nothing to do with all these UFO reports. You figured out what was going on last time with the phony vampire. Maybe you can find out what's going on now."

"What kind of UFO reports were they?" asked Einstein.

"The chief said a lot of people had called in saying that they were seeing mysterious lights in the sky. And the lights weren't planes or anything like that, because they kept changing shapes and moved too rapidly."

"Oh, is that all?" said Einstein. He pushed his glasses back. "Encounters of the first kind. I think the reason for all those calls is obvious."

Can you solve the mystery: What is causing the UFO reports?

"It may be obvious to you," said Mr. Freed. "But I have no idea what's happening. I do know that I have nothing to do with it, and neither does anyone from my movie."

"Well, that's not quite accurate," Einstein said. "It's your movie that's causing the UFO reports. Or rather, not your movie, but your movie *preview*."

"Now I really don't understand," Mr. Freed said in bewilderment. "How can my movie premiere cause UFO reports?"

"It's like this," explained Einstein. "You have bright spotlights moving back and forth on top of this theater, advertising the film. Their bright beams are going into the sky. But the night is very cloudy. So the light beams are being reflected off the bottom of the clouds. People in the distance can't see the beams. But they can see the reflected lights in the clouds move and change as the spotlights move."

"That must be right, Einstein," said Mrs. Anderson. "We Spartans don't usually see spotlights beaming around, so we aren't used to seeing the reflections of light from so far away."

"Thanks, kid," Mr. Freed chortled. "Remind me to give you a couple of tickets to see the movie again. I got to go now and call the chief and tell him that I figured out what his UFOs are. Won't he be embarrassed!"

"I guess Mr. Freed is now a real expert on out-of-this-world dishes," Einstein said.

"Huh?" said Dennis.

"Flying saucers," said Einstein.

2

The Case of the

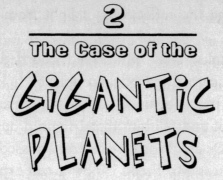
GIGANTIC PLANETS

Stanley Roberts was a good friend of Einstein Anderson, even though he was older and a junior at Sparta Senior High School. Stanley was very much interested in science and often invited Einstein to come over and see his inventions and experiments.

"This time I've really got something big in mind," Stanley said, pushing aside some flasks and test tubes on his laboratory table. "Let me show you my plans."

Stanley's "laboratory" was really the attic

room that his mom and dad had permitted him to use for his experiments. It was in its usual messy state. Bunsen burners, glassware, aquariums, small animal cages, and half-finished models were everywhere. It looked like a junk shop, but Stanley claimed it was all scientific apparatus.

"Something really big," asked Einstein, "like the giant ants or the green monster that you were going to send for through the mail?"

"Those were just silly mistakes," Stanley said, brushing back his black hair, which kept falling into his eyes. "This is different. It's really scientific. And you can help me construct it and share in the profits."

"Help you? How?" Einstein asked cautiously. "You're not still thinking of making an exercise machine, I hope. It worked fine when I used it. But when you sat down in that machine, the gears jammed. By the time I got it fixed and you got out, your muscles were so sore you couldn't play baseball for a week."

"No, no," said Stanley impatiently. "This is something completely different. You've been to a planetarium, haven't you?"

13

"Isn't that an all-star show?" Einstein asked him innocently.

"Well, you know how crowded the planetarium gets," Stanley said, ignoring Einstein's joke. "Can you imagine how much money we can make when I open a planetarium in my basement and charge admission?"

"Are you kidding?" said Einstein. "Do you know how difficult and expensive it is to construct a planetarium? Why, the star projector alone can cost thousands of dollars."

"This won't be that kind of planetarium," Stanley admitted. "It will really be just the solar system in the middle of the basement with star photos around the walls. The main attraction will be the sun and the planets."

"That reminds me of a joke, Stanley. Do you know what the little planet said when it went out of its orbit?"

"Huh?" said Stanley.

"'Look, Ma, no gravities!'"

Stanley groaned. "Forget those terrible

jokes," he said. "Look at this advertisement I'm going to answer and tell me if this isn't the best idea I've ever had."

"Right," said Einstein, looking at the magazine Stanley handed him. "I see you're still using authoritative scientific journals for your science ideas. *Thrilling Science Fiction Stories* is a great magazine for finding real science advertisements."

"Just read the ad," Stanley said warningly.

"O.K.," Einstein said hastily. He read the advertisement slowly. Then he looked up at Stanley. "This is an advertisement for scale models of Earth, the other planets of the solar system, and the sun."

"That's right. Isn't it a great idea? They'll send me an eight-inch-diameter model of Earth along with detailed plans for the sun and all the other planets to scale. I'll build the models exactly and then place them in my basement, using the same scale for their distances from the sun. Then I'll use large photos of the stars for the walls. It'll be spectacular!"

"Let me get this straight," said Einstein.

"You plan to build a scale model of the solar system, put it in your basement, and charge admission to see it?"

"You got it," Stanley said happily.

"I've got it," said Einstein, "but I don't think you have. Your idea is interesting. But it will never work."

Can you solve the mystery: What's wrong with Stanley's plans to build a model of the solar system in his basement?

"I don't see why not," Stanley said. "It shouldn't be too difficult to make models of the sun and the other planets. We can use clay or something like that for the models."

"You'll need an awful lot of clay," said Einstein. "Let's say that Earth is represented by an eight-inch globe. Earth is about eight thousand miles in diameter, so on that scale one inch equals one thousand miles. Jupiter, the largest planet in the solar system, is more than eighty-eight thousand miles in diameter. A model of Jupiter built to the same scale as the model of Earth would have to be eighty-eight inches in diameter, more than seven feet across."

"Uh-oh," said Stanley. "I forgot to check into the sizes of the planets."

"It's not even with the planets that you'd have the most to worry about," said Einstein. "It's the sun. The sun's diameter is more than eight hundred and sixty thousand miles. That means a scale model of the sun would be eight hundred and sixty inches across, more than seventy-one feet."

"I'll never get that into my basement," Stanley said, "but maybe we can find a hall that's big enough."

"Forget it," said Einstein. "Even if you did find a hall big enough for the models, it would still be too small to place them away from the sun in the same scale. Earth is ninety-three million miles from the sun. It would have to be ninety-three thousand inches away from the sun, or more than one mile away."

"I told you I had a big idea," Stanley said sadly.

"You have no idea how big," Einstein said. "Earth is one of the planets that's closest to the sun. But the most distant planet on average is Pluto. It's three thousand six hundred and seventy million miles from the Sun. On the same scale as the model of Earth you would have to place Pluto nearly seven hundred *miles* away!"

"Wow!" exclaimed Stanley. "How wrong can I be!"

"Cheer up," said Einstein. "Nothing is all wrong. Even a broken clock is right twice a day."

3

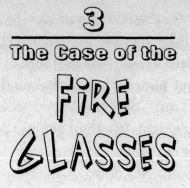

The Case of the
FiRE
GLASSES

Einstein was setting up the materials to do an experiment on water purification in the science laboratory at school when he saw Pat and Herman look in at the doorway. Pat Burns was not very high on Einstein's favorite-person list. In fact, Pat was Einstein's least favorite classmate.

Pat's nickname was Pat the Brat, but nobody called him that to his face. He was too big and mean to tangle with. Pat's friend, Herman, was not much higher on Einstein's list. Herman was almost as big and mean as

Pat. Einstein could stand up to Pat and Herman if he had to, but he usually tried to handle them by outthinking them.

Einstein turned his back to the door when Pat called out, "Say, would you look who's in the science lab! It's that genius, Mr. Four-eyed Einstein Anderson. I wonder what kind of experiment he's doing."

"Yeah, Pat. I wonder what experiment Einstein's doing," said Herman.

"That's what I just said, Herman!"

"Yeah, Pat, that's what you just said."

"Forget it, Herman. Let's go over and check out what Einstein's doing," Pat said.

Pat and Herman walked over to where Einstein was working. Pat said, "Now that looks very interesting, what you're doing, Einstein. Why don't you explain how it works to my pal Herman? Herman is very interested in science."

"Yeah," said Herman, "Herman is very interested in science."

"Sure," Einstein said agreeably. "What would you like to know?"

"Huh?" Herman said. He turned to Pat. "What would I like to know?"

"Say whatever's on your mind, Herman!" Pat exclaimed.

"If Herman said what was on his mind, he'd be speechless," Einstein murmured.

"Huh?" said Herman.

Pat threw up his arms and shouted, "Herman, don't you remember what we were talking about in the hall? You know. About Einstein's glasses. Remember?"

"Oh, yeah, I know that," said Herman. "I just didn't know that you wanted me to do it now."

"Yes, Herman," Pat said in exasperation. "Do it now. While I go out and get a drink in the hall." Pat turned away and went out the door, leaving Herman and Einstein staring at each other.

There was a long silence, and then Einstein spoke. "Well, I've really enjoyed this conversation with you, Herman, but I think I'll get back to my experiment now."

Herman nodded. Then he said, "Wait a

minute. I'm interested in your eyeglasses. Can I see them?"

"You want to see my glasses?" Einstein asked. "Is there any particular reason?"

"I'm thinking of getting eyeglasses myself," Herman said.

"Right," said Einstein. "I'm wearing my eyeglasses now, so you go right ahead and look at them all you want. And while you're looking, I'll just continue with my experiment."

"No, that's not what I mean," said Herman. "I'd like you to take off your eyeglasses and show them to me in the sunlight by the window over there."

Einstein stared at Herman. Pat and Herman must be up to some trick or other, he thought. But I'm curious to see what it is.

"O.K.," said Einstein, walking over to the window. "Here are my glasses." Einstein removed his glasses and held them up to Herman. The bright sun glinted on the lenses and sent reflections all over the room.

Herman took the eyeglasses. Then he pointed through the window and said, "Look

down there, Einstein. Isn't that your brother, Dennis?"

Einstein looked out through the window. "I can't see Dennis without my glasses," Einstein said. "I'm nearsighted and things far away look blurry. If you've finished examining my glasses, I'd be glad to look."

Einstein turned to reach for his glasses and was startled by what he saw. There was a fire in the wastebasket near the window where Herman was standing, and Pat was coming into the room with Ms. Taylor, the science teacher.

"I told you Einstein was starting a fire," Pat said to Ms. Taylor. "He was using his eyeglasses like a magnifying lens and getting the paper to burn. It's a lucky thing Herman and me saw him. I told Herman to take his glasses away, and I went to get you."

Ms. Taylor filled a flask with water and poured it on the fire to put it out. Then she turned to Einstein. "Is that true, Einstein? I can hardly believe you would be so careless as to deliberately start a fire."

"I didn't start the fire with my eyeglasses," said Einstein. "Pat or Herman must have started it with a match while I was looking out the window."

"Herman and I saw you starting the fire," Pat said. "And that's two against one."

"But I can prove that you're lying," Einstein said.

Can you solve the mystery: How can Einstein
prove that Pat and Herman are not telling the
truth?

"You wear glasses, don't you?" asked Pat.

"Yes," answered Einstein.

"Well, then you could have started a fire with them. Just like starting a fire with a magnifying glass."

"That would be impossible with my glasses," said Einstein.

"What makes your eyeglasses so different?" Pat said sneeringly.

"You see, I'm nearsighted," Einstein said. "And eyeglasses for nearsighted people are made with double concave lenses. The lenses spread light rays apart rather than concentrate them. That means that if you held my glasses in the sunlight you wouldn't get the concentrated spot of light that you would get with a magnifying lens. You could never use eyeglasses for nearsighted people to start fires. Eyeglasses made for *farsighted* people are like magnifying lenses, double convex. They can be used to concentrate light and to start a fire."

"Well, what have you got to say for yourselves?" Ms. Taylor asked Pat and Herman.

"It was Pat's fault," Herman said. "I could never think of an idea like that."

"Right," said Einstein. "You might say that when it came to my eyeglasses Pat made a *spectacle* of himself."

4
The Case of the
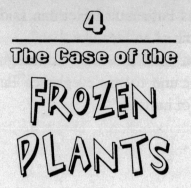

an you come over this afternoon, Einstein?" Margaret asked over the phone. "We can go sledding down the hill in back of my house, then have some hot chocolate and work on our science projects."

"I thought you had to do some chores today," Einstein said.

"I do," answered Margaret. "I'm going to go to City Hall this morning to get a license for Nova, and then I have a few things that maybe you can help me with this afternoon."

Nova was Margaret's dog, a black-and-white springer spaniel.

"Are you getting Nova a license?" Einstein asked innocently. "I didn't know she was old enough to drive."

Margaret laughed. "Don't tell me any more dog jokes," she said. "I don't have any time."

"O.K.," said Einstein. "But did you hear what happened at the flea circus? A dog came along and stole the show."

"Einstein!"

"I'll be over right after lunch," Einstein said. "As the frankfurter said when the dog bit him, it's a dog-eat-dog world. See you this afternoon."

After lunch Einstein walked over to Margaret's house. There was a lot of snow on the ground, and it was very cold. The weather prediction was for several days of subfreezing temperatures.

Einstein tried to pack some of the snow together to make a snowball, but the snow was too cold and dry and didn't stick. Einstein took off his gloves and made a snowball with his bare hands. He knew that his body heat would melt some of the snow and that the wet snow would make a better snowball.

When he had packed a good snowball, Einstein went into a full pitching motion and tried to hit a nearby tree. The snowball hit the tree trunk dead center, surprising Einstein so much that he tried again with another snowball. This time the snowball didn't even come close to the tree. Einstein's hands were now too cold for still another try, so he put his gloves back on and continued on his way to Margaret's house.

Margaret Michaels was Einstein's class-mate and good friend. Margaret was about as tall as Einstein and good at sports. Science was also her favorite subject. She and Einstein were always working on science experiments together and talking about important things like space travel, undersea life, and which one of them was the better scientist and baseball player.

When Einstein arrived at Margaret's house, she wanted to go right out and go sledding.

"I'm too cold," objected Einstein. "Let's have some hot chocolate and then we can go."

"Sure," agreed Margaret. "While I'm making the chocolate, you can help me do some of my inside chores. Then when we go out, you can help me do an outside chore."

"What would you like me to do?" Einstein asked agreeably. His hands were so cold that he was happy to do anything as long as he could stay inside the house for a while and warm up.

"First I'd like you to feed the tropical fish, then feed Orville and Wilbur. I've already fed Nova." Orville and Wilbur were Margaret's two cats. Margaret hadn't named her tropical fish yet.

"No sooner said than done." Einstein went into Margaret's room and sprinkled a pinch of fish food on the water of the aquarium. Then he went back into the kitchen and began to open a can of cat food. "I hope the outside chore is as easy to do as the inside chores," he said.

"That will be a little more difficult," Margaret admitted. "But I really have to get it done this afternoon, especially with all the cold weather coming."

"What do you have to do?" asked Einstein, spooning out equal parts of the cat food into two dishes.

"I have to clean off the snow from my bulb garden," answered Margaret.

"Oh? Are you doing some planting in the middle of winter?"

"Don't be funny, Einstein. I'm really worried about my daffodil bulbs. I planted them this fall, and I'm looking forward to seeing them blossom this spring."

"You can't plant any more bulbs this time of year," said Einstein, looking puzzled. "Why would you want to clean off the snow?"

"That should be obvious," said Margaret. "I want to make sure that the bulbs I did plant live through to the spring. Getting them out from under the snow will help keep them from freezing."

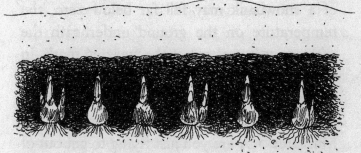

Einstein pushed back his glasses, which were slipping down. "I have a much better way of keeping your bulbs from freezing," he said. "And this way won't be nearly as difficult."

Can you solve the mystery: What's the easy way that Einstein knows to protect the bulbs from the cold weather?

"What could be easier than scraping off the snow covering?" asked Margaret.

"Not scraping off the snow," Einstein answered.

"What would you do to protect the bulbs?"

"The snow will protect the bulbs," explained Einstein. "Most people associate snow with cold," he continued, "but snow is a very good insulator of plants and animals in the soil. Even though the temperature on top of a snowbank may fall far below zero, the temperature on the ground underneath the snow stays just about at the freezing mark. In fact, snow acts to keep the ground temperature constant despite changes in the weather."

"Are you sure about that?" asked Margaret. "Or are you just trying to get out of doing a chore?"

"Would I lie about science?" Einstein laughed. "No, seriously, snow really is a good insulator because of all the dead air spaces it contains. In cold mountainous places small rodents can stay active during the winter under the snow. It never gets too cold for them there. But without the snow cover they would freeze in a short time."

"I never knew that about snow," Margaret said.

"Right," said Einstein. "Snow is easier to understand than any other kind of weather."

"Why is that?" Margaret asked.

"Because you can see the drift," said Einstein.

5

The Case of the

COUNTLESS STARS

"Einstein, would you help me with my homework?" asked Dennis. Dennis was in the third grade in Sparta Elementary School. He often asked Einstein to help him with his homework, particularly with science. It was easier to get Einstein's help, Dennis thought, than to look up the answer in his textbook.

"I hope the work isn't dull," answered Einstein. "The only person who hopes for dull work is a knife sharpener."

"Ha, ha," Dennis said politely. "Now can you help me?"

38

"For sure," said Einstein. He knew that his younger brother could look up the answers to many of the questions he asked, but he enjoyed teaching Dennis and acting like an older brother. "But remember that if you work in a pickle factory, all work and no play makes you a *dill* boy."

"Ugh." Dennis shuddered. "No more jokes, or I'll go crazy."

"You know that a crazy pickle is a daffy dill," Einstein said. "Sorry about that. What kind of homework do you want help with?"

"I'm doing a report about the stars," said Dennis. "I thought we could use your telescope in the backyard tonight, and you could point out some interesting stars and tell me about them."

"I'll be happy to set up my telescope tonight," Einstein said. "It's been a few weeks since I last observed. Do you have any questions we could go over before then?"

"Yes," said Dennis. "My teacher said that the sun is a star, and it looks so big and bright because it is so close. But are any of the stars bigger or brighter than the sun?"

39

"There are plenty of stars brighter and larger than the sun," Einstein answered. "Just in our own Milky Way galaxy, astronomers think that there are one hundred billion stars. That's about two dozen stars for each person living on the Earth. If you were just to count these stars at a rate of one per second, twenty-four hours a day, it would take you more than three thousand years to finish counting."

"I don't think I have that much time," said Dennis. "My test is Tuesday. Is the sun the smallest of these stars?"

"Not at all," Einstein said. "Our sun is a medium-size star that is medium bright. Imagine that all the stars are an equal distance from Earth. Suppose the sun were then as bright as a candle. Some stars would be as bright as a powerful lighthouse beacon. Other stars would be as dim as a glowworm."

"Are the brightest stars the biggest stars?" Dennis asked.

"Not necessarily," answered Einstein. "Some very large stars are not so bright, and some very bright stars are not so large. The largest stars are called giants or supergiants. A star named Betelgeuse—I call it Beetle Juice—is two hundred and fifty million miles across. If it were in the place of our sun, it would extend out past Earth's orbit. On the other hand, a star called Sirius B is only twenty-four thousand miles across, smaller than some of the planets."

"All those numbers are really interesting," Dennis said. "But I'd rather just look at the stars."

"People like to look at the stars because they're so heavenly," said Einstein. "O.K. Right after dinner I'll set up the telescope, and I'll show you Beetle Juice and some other stars."

It was dark and cold when the boys went into the backyard after dinner. While Einstein was setting up his telescope, he pointed out some of the winter constellations to Dennis.

"Those three bright stars close together in a row form the belt of Orion. Orion, the hunter, is the most interesting constellation in the winter sky. Betelgeuse is the very bright reddish star above and to the left of the belt. Rigel is the name of the brilliant blue-white star below and to the right."

"Can we see them through the telescope?" Dennis asked.

"Right," said Einstein. "I'll also show you a great cloud of gas, called a nebula, in Orion."

"Great," Dennis said. "The night is so clear! There must be a million stars out."

"Do you think so?" asked Einstein. "Why don't you count the stars you can see without a telescope just in that part of the sky in and around the constellation Orion."

"O.K.," said Dennis. "But it may take a while."

After a number of minutes Dennis said, "I've already counted more than a thousand stars. But I'm sure I can see at least a million. I can see as many stars as there are grains of sand on a beach."

"That's a beautiful thought, Dennis. But the truth is that you must have just been dreaming," said Einstein. "In fact, I don't think you counted to more than a thousand at all."

Can you solve the mystery: How did Einstein know that Dennis really couldn't have counted the stars near Orion?

"How do you know, Einstein?" Dennis asked. "Just because it didn't take me so long to count to one thousand? Suppose I was counting by tens and just looking at bunches of stars."

"That's not the reason," said Einstein. "You can see about one million stars with my small telescope. But using only your eyes, you can see only about two thousand stars. You could easily count that many in an hour or less. In and around Orion there are fewer than one hundred stars that you can see without a telescope."

"Then why did you tell me there were so many stars?" Dennis demanded.

"Those are the stars that we can see with our most powerful telescopes. And even then astronomers have to make just an estimate of the number of stars that are too faint to be seen."

"So the stars really are like grains of sand," said Dennis.

"Even more than the number of grains of sand on a beach," Einstein said. "There are many millions of other galaxies besides our own Milky Way galaxy. And each of the galaxies contains hundreds of millions of stars."

"Wow!" Dennis exclaimed. "Do you think there are strange beings living somewhere out there? And that they may someday come to Earth to visit?"

"I think I know what they'll say if they come," said Einstein.

"What?"

"We didn't *planet* this way!"

6

The Case of the

WIND-SWEPT STAMPS

One day in the early spring Einstein's sixth-grade class went on a field trip to the nearby seashore. Einstein brought along a magnifying lens, a small microscope, a number of plastic jars in which to collect specimens, and a ball. To make sure he wouldn't go hungry, Einstein had packed two peanut butter and jelly sandwiches, a bag of potato chips, an apple, and a can of orange juice.

Margaret brought a pair of binoculars for bird-watching and a camera. Besides sandwiches, Margaret had packed some home-baked chocolate-chip cookies for her friends. She also brought a Frisbee.

Margaret and Einstein sat in the back of the school bus along with their friends Sally and Mike. They were munching on the chocolate-chip cookies and looking at some stamps that Sally had brought along to show them.

"This is a block of eight stamps that I just bought for my collection," Sally said. "The stamps commemorate the exploration of the moon, the space shuttle *Columbia,* and other science events. I thought you'd be interested in seeing them."

Einstein took out his magnifying lens to examine the stamps more closely. "They're really nice," he said. "Look at these, Margaret."

Margaret was examining the stamps when Pat and Herman came over.

"What have you got there?" asked Pat. "Give them here."

"How about asking politely?" said Margaret.

Pat clenched his fist, then thought better

47

of it. The only time he had picked on Margaret, she had taken him by surprise and hauled off and socked him. He had gone around with a black eye for a week.

"Herman, you ask," ordered Pat.

"Sure, Pat," said Herman. "What do you want me to ask?"

"Never mind," said Sally. "You can take a look at my stamps. Just handle them carefully. I wouldn't want them to be bent. Let me put them in a plastic envelope."

"These must cost a lot of money," Pat said, examining the stamps. "You better be careful where you keep them." He looked thoughtful. "Let's go back to our seats, Herman," he said.

"Doesn't Herman ever do anything without being told to by Pat?" Mike said.

"Herman is going to leave his brain to science," said Einstein. "Every little bit helps."

When the bus arrived at the shore, small groups of kids scattered in all directions. One group was going to check on the beach erosion that had taken place over the winter. Another group was going to look to see how people's activities affected the ecology of the beach area. Einstein, Margaret, Sally, and Mike were going to study intertidal communities made up of barnacles, rockweed, and mussels.

After working for about an hour, some of the kids began to spread blankets on the beach and eat their lunches.

"Everyone seems to be eating," Einstein said, "and I'm starved. Let's quit working for a while and take a lunch break."

"I agree," said Mike. "Even cannibals have to break for lunch. They like baked beings."

"That cannibal joke is in poor taste," Einstein observed.

"Ugh," said Sally.

While they were sitting on a blanket and eating, Margaret took out her binoculars and began to look at the birds. She identified several kinds of gulls, sandpipers, terns, and a petrel. Einstein pointed out how the gulls had to take off facing the wind like an airplane. "You can see how their footprints lead down to the water into the wind," he said.

After lunch they decided to have a catch with the Frisbee, but the strong wind kept

blowing it off course. Some of the other kids
in the class who were still sitting and eating
lunch made pointed suggestions about the
Frisbee when it spun into their sandwiches.

"Let's go behind those trees on top of the
dune," said Margaret. "It should be less windy
there."

It wasn't. After climbing a tree to retrieve the Frisbee for the third time, Einstein remarked, "Now I understand how trees become petrified. The wind makes them rock."

"That does it," said Margaret. "I'd rather get back to the seashore and work than watch Einstein climb trees and make corny jokes."

Naturally, as soon as they started to walk back, the wind died down. They were sliding down the dunes when Margaret spotted Pat and Herman going through their things. They ran the rest of the way to the blanket. Pat and Herman stood up when they arrived.

"What are you two doing?" Margaret demanded.

"Trying to save Sally's stamps, that's what," said Pat. "Herman and me were walking past when we saw the wind start to blow things off the blanket. I know how expensive those stamps are, so we came over to make sure they wouldn't blow away. I took out the stamps to make sure they were safe. But the wind suddenly blew them out of my hands and into the water.

"That's a likely story," Sally said. "You probably just wanted to steal the stamps. Then when you saw us coming you made up that phony tale."

"What do you mean?" Pat said. "I even ran into the water to try to catch the stamps. You can see my shoes and jeans are wet."

"But it isn't even windy now," said Mike.

"But it was windy just a few minutes ago," Pat said. "You ought to thank me for trying to rescue the stamps rather than blame me for stealing them."

"That story is just a big bag of wind," said Einstein. "You just blew your excuse."

Can you solve the mystery: How does Einstein know that Pat is not telling the truth?

"Maybe Pat *is* telling the truth," Sally said. "After all, we didn't see what happened to the stamps."

"Pat made up that story about the wind blowing the stamps into the water," said Einstein.

"But how can you be sure?" Mike asked.

"Because of the gulls," Einstein said.

"What!?" exclaimed Pat. "Don't tell me that a little bird told you!"

"In a way," said Einstein. "You see, the gulls' tracks led down to the water when they took off. Now gulls take off into the wind. The wind was blowing hard, that's true. But it was blowing off the water *toward* land. So if the wind blew the stamps out of your hand, they would have been blown up toward the dunes, not into the water."

"I was just kidding," Pat said sullenly, and he reached into his pocket. "Here are your old stamps. I wasn't going to really steal them. Let's get out of here, Herman. These kids can't take a joke."

Watching Pat walk away, Einstein observed, "You know, if Pat ever had his conscience removed, it would be a very minor operation."

7

The Case of the

DEAFENING

SOUNDS

I just thought of an invention that will help put an end to the world energy crisis," said Stanley. His long black hair fell over his eyes, and he impatiently pushed it back. "I don't know why nobody has thought of it before."

"You go right ahead and invent it," said Einstein. "After all, the world laughed at Thomas Edison. They laughed at Eli Whitney. They laughed at Peter Snerd."

"What did Peter Snerd invent?" asked Stanley.

"Nothing," Einstein said, "but they sure laughed at him."

"Einstein!" Stanley exclaimed warningly. "This is no laughing matter."

"Sorry," Einstein said. "It's just that I *ear* such awful *corn* these days."

"Ohh," Stanley groaned. "Will you please be serious and listen to my idea? I didn't ask you to come up to my laboratory for nothing. This is going to be a great occasion. You will be the witness to a great experiment. An experiment that will show the way to great energy savings."

Einstein looked around Stanley's "laboratory." It was just as messy as always. There didn't seem to be any new weird contraptions lurking in the corners.

"What kind of experiment are you going to do?" Einstein asked cautiously. "I hope I don't have to be a subject. Every time you try a new invention, something goes wrong. That super-stick glue that you made your dad use to mend his glasses only lasted till he went out of the house."

"Well, how was I to know that the glue broke down chemically in sunlight?" Stanley said.

"It wasn't just that his glasses came apart," Einstein said. "The glue sure had a powerful odor. All the cats in the neighborhood followed him to work, meowing like crazy."

"Let's just forget about that," said Stanley. "All you have to do while I do this experiment is watch." He walked over to his stereo and turned up the sound.

"It would be easier to hear what you're saying," said Einstein, "if you turned down the volume of your stereo a bit. I like to listen to rock, but you're blasting it so loud that I can't hear you."

"But that's my experiment," Stanley said in a loud voice. "The rock music that kids are playing all over the country will now be used to help the energy shortage. Instead of having parents complain about the noise, they'll urge their kids to play the music louder."

"That'll be the day," said Einstein. "You better explain before I go deaf."

"You know that sound is a form of energy," Stanley said. "And rock music is a very loud sound. Do you get it?"

"The only thing I'm getting is a headache," Einstein said. "I know that sound is energy and that rock is loud. So what?"

"Aha!" Stanley exclaimed. "Even the great Einstein Anderson doesn't understand the connection. I've done it at last! A major breakthrough!" Stanley started to jump up and down in his best imitation of a mad scientist.

"Be cool," advised Einstein. "Maybe you'd better cross your stereo with a refrigerator. Will you please explain to me as simply as you can what you're talking about."

"Gladly," Stanley said. "Like all great inventions, it's simple. Do you see this glass of water that I've placed in front of my stereo's speakers? That glass of water will prove that my idea works. I'll place a thermometer in the water and check the temperature. Then I'll play loud music at the water while I monitor the changes in the water's temperature. If my theory is correct, the sound energy of the music will raise the temperature of the water. As the water gets hotter, we can use the hot water in all kinds of ways to save energy."

Einstein looked at Stanley for a long time and then pushed back his glasses with one finger. "You can't be serious," he said.

"I certainly am serious," Stanley said.

"Sound is a form of energy, right? And heat is a form of energy, too. All I'm proposing is to use some of the waste energy that music gives off and use it to heat water. Is there anything scientifically wrong with that?"

"Well, everything you say is true," replied Einstein. "But, unfortunately, your idea will never work."

Can you solve the mystery: What is wrong with Stanley's idea of using loud music to heat water and save energy?

"I think you're wrong this time, Einstein," Stanley declared. "I know that sound is energy and that it can be turned into heat."

"That part is true," said Einstein. "The problem is the amount of heat that sound energy can produce. You see, when a loud-speaker produces a sound, it puts out only a tiny fraction of the amount of energy needed to make the sound in the first place. In fact, all the sounds around us, from the buzzing of a bee to the roar of a jet engine, have tiny amounts of energy compared with any source of heat, such as an electric lightbulb or a candle."

"Will the water in the glass get hot at all?" asked Stanley.

"Well, if you keep the rock music blasting away steadily, the temperature of the water should go up to about fifty degrees Celsius, or about one hundred and twenty degrees Fahrenheit. In about ten years."

"That's not good," Stanley said disconsolately.

"It's better than if you carried the glassful of water around with you on a subway train,"

Einstein said. "That would take you only one thousand years of traveling on the train to get the water up to fifty degrees Celsius."

"I guess I can lower the volume," Stanley said, turning down the dial.

"Say, do you know what kind of rock ghosts like?" Einstein asked.

"What?" Stanley said.

"Tombstones," said Einstein. "I think I better be going now."

8

The Case of the

MOON JUMPS

ow about having a scale that shows what you would weigh on the moon?" Einstein suggested to Margaret. "We can use the balance scale from the school nurse's room. Then we can write the moon-weight figures on cardboard and tape them to the scale."

"That's a good idea," replied Margaret. "We'll just divide each of the weight numbers on the scale by six. That will give us the weights on the moon."

"Right," said Einstein. "The moon's gravitational pull is only one-sixth as strong as Earth's. So a person would weigh only one-sixth as much on the moon as on Earth."

"That's a great way to lose weight," said Margaret. "The only trouble is that your mass remains the same, so that you look the same as you do on Earth."

"Let's review what we have so far for the Lunar Olympics. We have a weight-lifting contest, and we'll label the weights with numbers one-sixth of their Earth weight—"

"Won't Pat be happy when he can lift a few hundred pounds over his head!" interrupted Margaret.

"Pat is already so bigheaded that he can't find an aspirin that will fit him," Einstein agreed. "He's always trying to push himself forward by patting himself on the back."

"Don't get started telling jokes," said Margaret. "We have to stage the Lunar Olympics of the year 2100 at Moon Base I for our class next week. That means we have to complete the plans today so we know what materials we'll need."

"The materials better not cost too much,"

said Einstein. "After all, the moon itself is only worth a dollar."

"What?" Margaret asked bewilderedly.

"The moon has four quarters, so it's only worth…"

"Never mind, Einstein! Just get on with the plans."

"Sorry about that. Let me see. Besides the weight lifting, we have a shot-put contest. Instead of a heavy iron ball, we'll use a baseball painted gray and labeled with a weight six times as heavy as it really is."

"We can have two contests with the ball," said Margaret, "a distance throw and a height throw. Then we can compare the results with a real shot-put contest on Earth."

"Say, if an athlete gets athlete's foot, do you know what an astronaut gets?" Einstein asked.

"I'm sure you'll tell me," said Margaret.

"An astronaut gets mistletoe. Get it? Missile-toe."

"I got it," said Margaret, "but I hope it's not catching."

"I wish you'd stop joking around." Einstein

laughed. "You're making me into a moon insect—a lunatic. A *lunar tick*. Why aren't you laughing, Margaret?"

"Just get on with it, Einstein," Margaret said, trying to keep from smiling. "Suppose we have a walking race over a hundred-yard course. Only we'll really make the course sixteen yards long. Then we can have a high-jump bar labeled six times higher than it really is."

"That's not what would happen on the real moon, Margaret," said Einstein.

"Are you still joking?" asked Margaret. "If you can throw a weight six times as high and six times as far on the moon as you can on Earth, then you should be able to walk six times as fast and jump six times as high as you can on Earth."

"This is no joke," said Einstein. "Although it seems logical, it really isn't."

Can you solve the mystery: Why can't you walk six times faster and jump six times higher on the moon?

"You'll have to explain that," said Margaret.

"Right," said Einstein. "You see, when you walk on Earth, your body is raised up about one and a half inches with each step. But on the moon it will drop back more slowly than it does on Earth. On the moon you would be walking more slowly than you could walk on Earth."

"I think I understand," Margaret said

slowly. "But surely a high jumper could jump over a bar six times higher on the moon."

"He could jump over a higher bar, but not six times higher," said Einstein. "The reason has to do with the way he lifts his feet and where his center of gravity is. Let's say that a high jumper is six feet tall. His center of gravity, the point where all his weight is concentrated, is about three and a half feet off the ground. To jump over a six-foot bar, he has to raise his center of gravity only two and a half feet. To clear the bar, he lifts his legs as far up as possible. That means that he really raised his center of gravity only two and a half feet to jump over the six-foot bar. So on the moon he wouldn't be able to jump over a thirty-six-foot-high bar."

"How high could he jump?" asked Margaret.

"He could jump six times the two and a half feet, about fifteen feet high. Then if he raised his legs upward the same as on Earth, he could clear another three and a half feet."

"That means he should be able to jump over a bar about eighteen and a half feet high," Margaret calculated. "That's still a pretty good jump."

"Oh, that's not so good," said Einstein. "I bet you I could jump across the room."

"Let's see you do it," said Margaret.

Einstein walked to the other side of the room and then jumped. "I told you I could jump across the room," he said.

9
The Case of the
SPEEDY ROWBOAT

Almost everyone in Einstein's sixth-grade class was going to be at Big Lake State Park the first Saturday in May. Einstein biked up with Margaret early in the morning. It was a beautiful sunny day.

"Look at those fluffy cumulus clouds," said Einstein. "They usually mean good weather."

"I can see that without looking at the clouds, Mr. Weatherman," said Margaret.

"A weatherman is someone everybody listens to but nobody believes," said Einstein.

"My forecast for today is clear and sunny with a fifty percent chance that I'm wrong."

Margaret laughed. "With a forecast like that, I'm sorry I didn't bring my umbrella."

"Margaret, can you tell me, if eight kids and six dogs were under an umbrella, how come none of them got wet?"

"The umbrella was a big one?"

"No. It just wasn't raining."

"Do you know the difference between an umbrella and a person who never stops talking?" asked Margaret.

"No," Einstein admitted.

"The umbrella can be shut up," said Margaret.

"Ouch," said Einstein. "I won't say another word. For a minute at least."

When they arrived at Big Lake, they were met by their friends Sally and Mike.

"Let's go down to the dock," said Mike. "We can rent a rowboat and row over to the other side of the lake."

"They just took the boats out of winter storage," said Sally. "And there aren't too many available. Most of the kids in our class are already rowing."

"Do you know where Chinese boats are stored for the winter?" asked Einstein. "In a *junk*yard."

They walked down to the dock. There were a number of rowboats on the lake and a small crowd of kids fishing off the side of the dock.

While Mike and Sally arranged for the boat rental, Einstein watched one of the rowboats on the lake. It was heading straight for another boat and narrowly missed hitting it. Einstein could see Pat and Herman rowing the first boat.

"Uh-oh," Einstein said. "It looks like Pat and Herman are playing dodge 'em with their rowboat. I wouldn't be surprised if they knocked somebody into the water."

"They'd better not pick on us," said Margaret. "Or I know someone's going to end up with a black eye."

Einstein nodded. He knew that Margaret had very little patience with Pat, and that Pat

usually picked on only the smallest members
of the class.

The four of them got into their boat and
began to row toward the other boats. Sally

and Mike each had an oar, while Einstein
and Margaret sat in the stern. It wasn't long
before they spotted Pat and Herman rowing
toward them.

"Look who's in that boat, Herman," shouted Pat. "It's my old pal Einstein Anderson! And naturally he's not rowing. He's too weak."

"You're the one who doesn't know how to row, Pat," said Einstein. "Your boat is going from side to side and nearly hitting everyone else's boat."

"That sounds like a challenge to me," said Pat. "I'm a better rower than you are any day. How about a race? Loser has to pay the boat rental for the winner."

"I don't think so," said Einstein. "It wouldn't be fair. We have four people in our boat and you have only two in yours."

"Come on, Einstein. Don't be chicken. Maybe you can use your brains to win. Ha, ha. You said science can help you do anything."

Einstein pushed back his glasses and thought for a moment. "O.K., Pat," he said. "I'll take one of the oars and Margaret will take the other. The first one in either boat who gets to the dock, jumps out, and runs to the boathouse at the end of the dock wins."

"But we'll never get to the dock before them," Margaret whispered to Einstein.

"Don't worry, I have an idea," Einstein whispered back. Then he said loudly, "Mike, as soon as we get close to the dock, you jump onto the dock and run over to the boathouse. That way we'll save time."

"But, Einstein," protested Margaret, "Pat heard your plans. He'll do the same thing and beat us to the boathouse."

"Trust me," said Einstein. "Pat will never get to the boathouse before Mike."

Can you solve the mystery: How does Einstein expect to beat Pat in the race?

"We'd better start rowing," said Margaret. "Pat is already on the way to the dock."

Einstein and Margaret scrambled into the seats next to the oars, and Mike and Sally went to the bow of the rowboat. Pat and Herman's boat was in the lead all the way to the dock. When their boat got within jumping range of the dock, Pat stood up and started to leap the rest of the way. But as he did so, his boat suddenly lurched backward, and Pat fell into the water with a loud splash.

"How did you know that was going to happen?" Mike asked when they stopped laughing.

"Because of a great scientist who lived three hundred years ago—Isaac Newton. Newton's third law of motion says that for every action there is an equal and opposite reaction. When Pat tried to jump from the boat to the dock, he pushed backward against the boat with his foot. His jump toward the dock was the action. The boat's movement away from the dock was the reaction. The distance between the boat and the dock widened, so Pat ended up in the water."

"So that's why you shouted our plans to me. You wanted Pat to overhear and copy what you said," said Mike.

"Right," said Einstein. "I figured that Pat would think that jumping was the special way I was going to beat him. You might say that Pat took a forward spring—and an early fall."

10
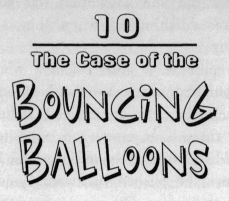
The Case of the
BOUNCING BALLOONS

The Spring Festival was a big event at Sparta Middle School. It was held the first Tuesday in May. The school gym was always decorated with balloons and streamers for the occasion. Each class had special exhibits and booths. There was to be a flower sale, a cake and cookie sale, and a used-book sale. The money would go to charity and to the school fund.

Einstein and Margaret had cooperated on an exhibit titled "Science and Sports." They had made posters showing how and why pitchers could throw a curve ball, what happened to a football when it was kicked, and how the knowledge of science could help athletes improve their athletic skills.

Einstein and Margaret were walking home from school the afternoon before the festival. It was a sunny, crisp spring day, and they had just had a baseball game in the school yard.

"Our exhibit will be the most popular at the festival," Margaret predicted. "We have posters on almost every kind of sport, including baseball, football, soccer, track, basketball, swimming, and a lot more."

"Right," Einstein agreed. "We even have posters on the noisiest and the quietest sports."

"Which are those?" Margaret asked.

"Bowling is the quietest sport because you can hear a pin drop," said Einstein. "And tennis is the noisiest sport because everyone raises a racket."

Margaret held her nose between her thumb and forefinger to show how much she appreciated Einstein's jokes. "Einstein," she said, "you're *joking* me to death."

Einstein immediately held his nose to show how much he appreciated Margaret's joke. "Truce?" he asked.

"Good idea," said Margaret. "To get back to the festival, I still don't understand why Ms. Paley, the art teacher, appointed Pat to the decorating committee. He's certain to make a mess of things."

"Maybe Ms. Paley thought she'd give Pat a fat chance to succeed. After all, he has a head to match."

Margaret laughed. "Well, Herman is the other kid on the decorating committee. What harm could Pat and Herman possibly do?"

When Einstein and Margaret went to school the next day, they found out. It was raining, and they had come to school on the early bus to put the finishing touches on their exhibit. When they opened the door to the gymnasium, they saw inflated balloons all over the floor and the exhibits. Ms. Paley was excitedly talking to another teacher.

When she saw Einstein and Margaret, she motioned them to come over.

"Can you believe what Pat and Herman did?" she asked angrily. "When I left the school yesterday afternoon, everything seemed to be

fine. Pat was really working, for a change. He had taped up all the streamers and was just about to put up the balloons."

"What happened?" asked Margaret.

"That's what I'd like to know," Ms. Paley said grimly. "Either Pat and Herman never put up the balloons at all or they decided to play games and knock them all down. But they're not going to get away with it. This time they're really going to be punished. I've just sent for them to come here and explain what happened."

A few minutes later the door to the gymnasium opened, and Pat and Herman came in. Pat looked around at the balloons all over the floor and started to shake his head. "I had nothing to do with this," he said. "When I left here, all the balloons were up. Someone must have knocked them down last night."

"Who was here when you left?" asked Ms. Paley.

"No one," said Pat. "The custodian locked the door to the school behind us. Herman, you were with me. Didn't we put all the balloons on the walls and the ceiling?"

"Sure, Pat," said Herman. "We didn't do nothing bad."

"Then how do you account for this mess?" Ms. Paley asked. "Do you expect me to believe that all the balloons just fell down by themselves?"

"Got me," said Pat, scratching his head.

"Excuse me, Pat," said Einstein. "But how did you put the balloons up, anyway? I can't see any tape on them."

"We used static electricity just like we learned in class," said Pat. "Herman and I rubbed the balloons on our sweaters and then put them on the walls or tossed them up on the ceiling. They really stuck great."

"Pat, you used science to help you!" said Einstein. "I'm really surprised."

"Yeah, and look where science got me," said Pat gloomily. "Deep in trouble."

"And science will get you out of trouble," said Einstein. "I think I know what happened with the balloons."

Can you solve the mystery: How can science get Pat out of trouble?

"How do you know what happened?" asked Ms. Paley. "You weren't here."

"But I did play baseball after school," said Einstein. "And it was a crisp day, very dry and sunny. And today is rainy."

"So what?" asked Ms. Paley. "How does that prove anything?"

"It has to do with static electricity," explained Einstein. "When Pat rubbed the balloons on his sweater yesterday, they became charged with static electricity very easily. Dry, crisp days are best for that. The charged balloons would have stuck very tightly to the ceiling or the walls."

"Then why did they come down?" asked Ms. Paley.

Pat and Herman glanced at each other uneasily as they waited for Einstein's answer.

"Well, the charge leaks out anyway," said Einstein. "And on damp days the charge leaves even more quickly. As soon as the balloons lose their charge, they are no longer attracted to the ceiling, and they fall."

Ms. Paley turned to Pat.

"Well, as long as it was just an accident, I

guess I can't blame you," she said. "But you and Herman better get all these balloons back up before the festival starts. And this time let Einstein and Margaret help you to make sure the balloons don't fall down."

"Sure, Pat," said Einstein. "*Stick* with me and I'll see what I can *glue* for you."

He's a sixth grade genius who knows so much
about science and nature that his friends call him Einstein.
Read all the adventures and solve the mysteries of science
with

by Seymour Simon
Illustrated by S.D. Schindler